Callie Cat, Ice Skater

Eileen Spinelli

Illustrated by

Anne Kennedy

SCHOLASTIC INC.
New York Toronto London Auckland
Sydney Mexico City New Delhi Hong Kong

For Bill Reiss and Moses Cardona
and the folks at John Hawkins and Associates.—E.S.

For Betsy.—A.K.

ISBN: 978-0-545-22644-8

12 11 10 9 8 7 6 5 4 3 2 1   9 10 11 12 13 14/0

Printed in the U.S.A.   40

First Scholastic printing, December 2009

The design is by Carol Gildar.

Winter was Callie's favorite season.
In winter she would go ice skating.
Callie loved ice skating.
She loved it more than chocolate cake.
More than her fuzzy red sweater.
Even more than going to the mall.

On weekend mornings Callie skated by day, when the sun was
bright and the wind sang through the tall stalks of thistle.

During the week she skated by night, when moonlight flowed silvery across her backyard pond and frost dusted the bench where she laced up her skates.

Whenever Callie skated,
she felt a melting sweetness.
A melting sweetness that had
no name.

Callie's friends Liza and May didn't care much for ice skating.
They were always trying to get Callie to do something else.
"Let's play Go Fish."
"Let's make bead necklaces."

Until they heard about the Honeybrook Ice Skating Contest.

"Look!" cried May, waving the flyer in Callie's face.

"It's a contest!" said Liza.

"Ice skating!"

"Prizes!"

"A one-year free pass to the Honeybrook Ice Rink!"

"New clothes!"

"A ride in a white limo!"

They showed the flyer to Callie's mother.

"Do you want to enter this ice skating contest?" her mother asked.

Before Callie could reply, May piped up: "Of course she does."

"She'd be a banana if she didn't," said Liza. And so it was settled.

On weekends, by day, Callie practiced ice skating.
"Do that spin again!" called May.

During the week Callie practiced by night.
"Be more graceful!" called Liza.

Finally the day of the contest arrived.
"Good luck," said her father.
"Just do your best," said her mother.

"Win!" said Liza.
"Win!" said May.

Soon came the announcement: "All contestants to the ice!"
The skaters filed out.
Callie tried to find her parents and friends in the crowd. She couldn't see them. But she could hear May shouting, "Careful on those spins!"
Callie was fifth in the line-up.

She watched the first four ice skaters. The first one danced a beautiful program. But on the last spin she fell.

The second girl twirled herself dizzy—smack into the lap of a judge.

The third got the giggles.

The fourth burst into tears.

Callie began to believe
she could win the contest.
    She thought of the prizes.
    A one-year pass to the
Honeybrook Ice Rink.
    New clothes.
    A ride in a white limo.
    She thought, "I'd be
a banana *not* to want all that."

Callie heard the
announcer call her name.

At last it was her turn.

She leaned into the music,

pushed off,

and glided across the ice.

She sailed.

She twirled.

Not one stumble.
Everyone cheered.

Callie watched the next three skaters.
Two of them were very good.

At last it was time for the judges to announce the winner.
Callie held her breath.

" . . . And the winner is—Maria Rivera!"

"You did your best," said Callie's mother.
"We're very proud of you," said her father.

"You must feel awful," whispered May. "Losing like that."
"She'd be a banana not to feel awful," said Liza.

That night Callie huddled under her covers.
Funny thing was, she didn't really feel very bad.
Or sad. Or terrible. Only tired.
Maybe she *was* a banana.

Go get em Callie!

Good Luck!

The next morning Callie went out to the pond.
The sun was bright.
The wind sang through tall stalks of thistle.
Callie put on her skates. She stood on the ice.

May wasn't there to watch her spins.
Liza wasn't there to tell her to be more graceful.
It was Callie ... only Callie ... by herself ... alone.

She began to slide across the frozen pond . . .

and skate . . .

and skate . . .

She began to feel something she hadn't felt for weeks.
It was back, and it was better than any prize. And her
sun-dazzled blades crisping across the ice gave her a more
wonderful ride than any white limo.

She knew that the melting sweetness came from doing what she loved.
Came not from winning, but doing.

The melting sweetness was the best prize of all.
And suddenly she knew the name for it.

Its name was joy.